The Three Bears ABC

An Alphabet Book

BY GRACE MACCARONE
ILLUSTRATED BY HOLLIE HIBBERT

www.av2books.com

Your AV² Media Enhanced book gives you a fiction readalong online. Log on to www.av2books.com and enter the unique book code from this page to use your readalong.

AV² Readalong Navigation

Go to **www.av2books.com**, and enter this book's unique code.

BOOK CODE

P261733

AV² by Weigl brings you media enhanced books that support active learning.

First Published by

ALBERT WHITMAN & COMPANY
Publishing children's books since 1919

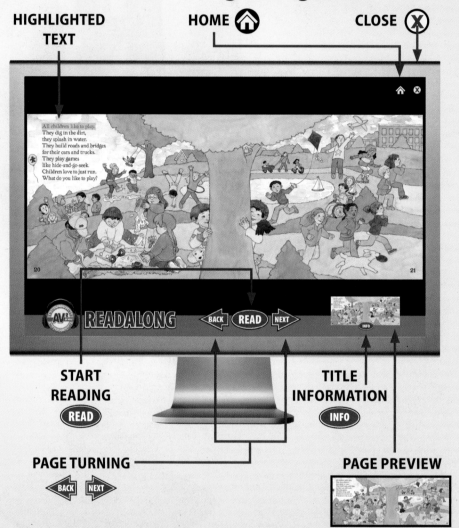

HIGHLIGHTED TEXT

HOME

CLOSE

START READING — READ

PAGE TURNING — BACK NEXT

TITLE INFORMATION — INFO

PAGE PREVIEW

Published by AV² by Weigl
350 5ᵗʰ Avenue, 59ᵗʰ Floor New York, NY 10118
Website: www.av2books.com   www.weigl.com

Copyright ©2014 AV² by Weigl

Printed in the United States of America in North Mankato, Minnesota
1 2 3 4 5 6 7 8 9 0 17 16 15 14 13

052013
WEP250413

Library of Congress Control Number: 2013940111

ISBN 978-1-62127-898-6 (hardcover)
ISBN 978-1-48961-481-0 (single-user eBook)
ISBN 978-1-48961-482-7 (multi-user eBook)

Text copyright ©2013 by Grace Maccarone.
Illustrations copyright ©2013 by Hollie Hibbert.
Published in 2013 by Albert Whitman & Company.

A is for alphabet.
And here it is . . .

A B C D E F G H
I J K L M N O P
Q R S T U V
W X Y Z

B is for bears.

There were three bears—
Mama Bear, Papa Bear,
and Baby Bear, who were in bed.

Then Mama Bear made breakfast—
big bowls of porridge.

5

is for cool.

The bears waited
for the hot porridge to cool.

So Papa put on his cap,
Mama her cape,
and Baby his coat.

D is for door.

They headed for the door.

8

And  is for exit.

Everyone exited.

F is for forest.

While their porridge cooled,
the bears walked in the forest,
where they sniffed fragrant flowers.

G is for girl.
named Goldilocks.

H

is for house.

Goldilocks saw the bears' happy house in the forest.

is for inside,
where Goldilocks went.

J is for just right.

The littlest bowl of porridge was just right. (The big bowl of porridge was too hot, and the medium bowl of porridge was too cold.)

15

**K** is for kitchen.

The bears kept their rocking chairs in the kitchen, where Goldilocks tried each one. One was too fast, one was too slow, and one was just right. Oops! It broke!

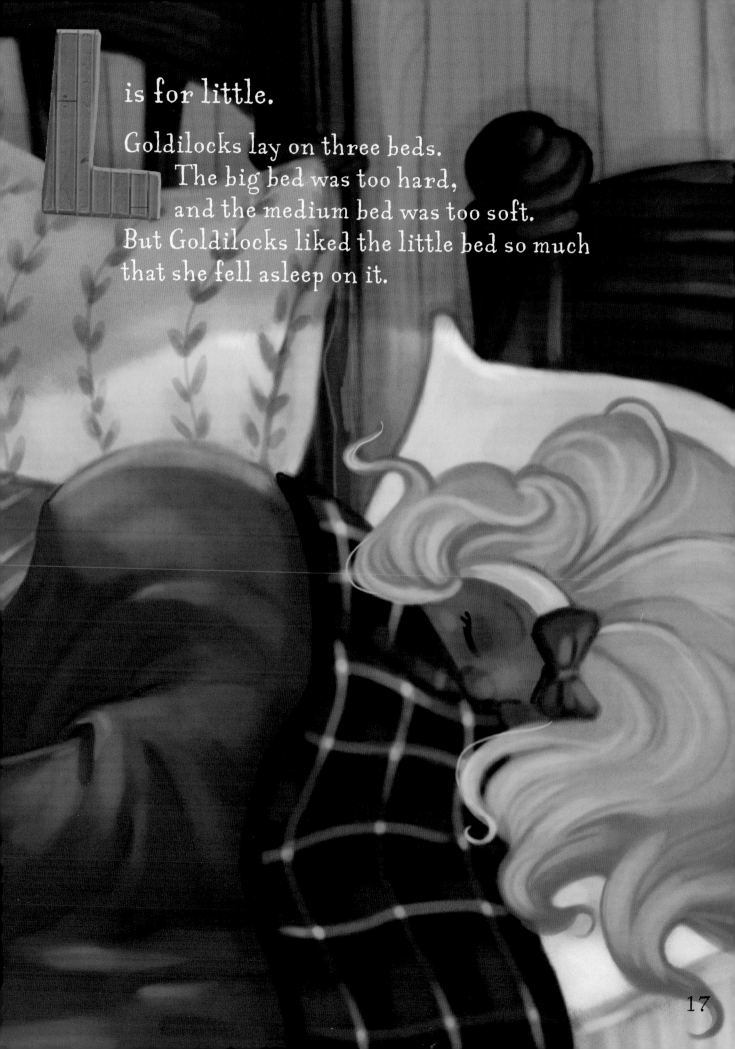

L is for little.

Goldilocks lay on three beds.
The big bed was too hard,
and the medium bed was too soft.
But Goldilocks liked the little bed so much
that she fell asleep on it.

M

is for mama.

Mama led her family back home.

N is for now.

The bears were hungry.
Grrr! They needed
their breakfast
NOW!

O is for open.

The bears found their front door open. How odd!

P is for Papa.

Papa Bear pointed to his bowl and said
"Someone has tasted my porridge."
Someone had tasted Mama Bear's porridge too.
And someone had tasted Baby Bear's porridge
and eaten it all up!

21

Q is for question.

Baby Bear asked this question: "Who ate my porridge?"

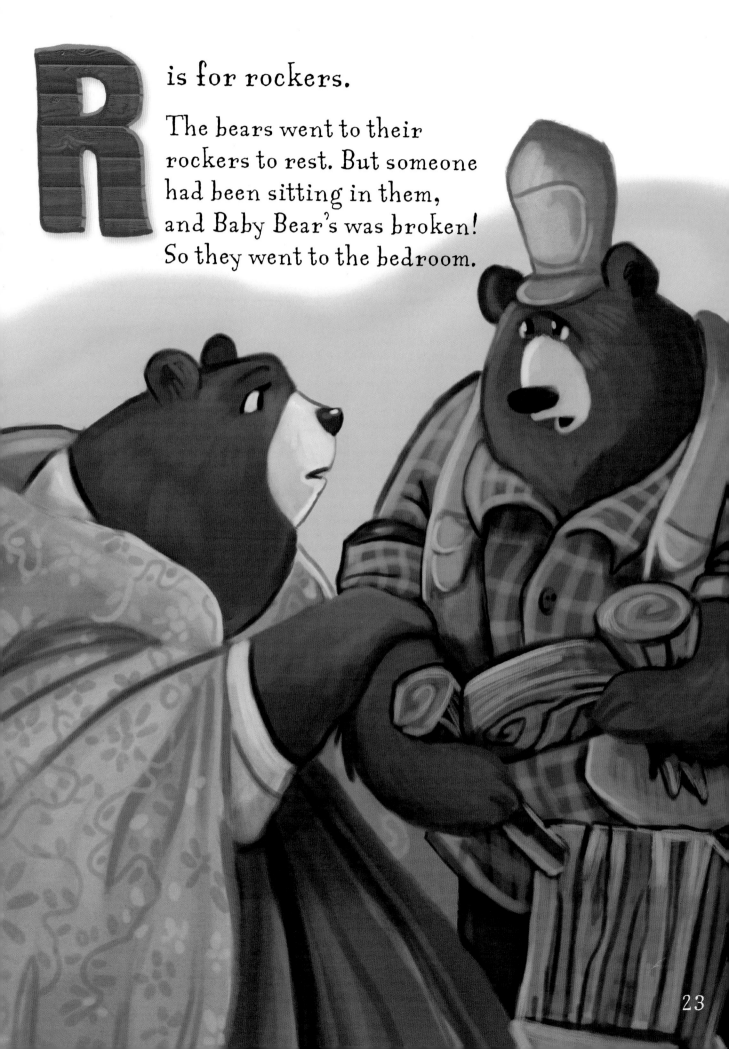

R is for rockers.

The bears went to their rockers to rest. But someone had been sitting in them, and Baby Bear's was broken! So they went to the bedroom.

23

S is for sleeping.

"Someone has been sleeping in my bed," said Papa.
"Someone has been sleeping in my bed," said Mama.
"Someone has been sleeping in my bed," said Baby.

T is for ta-dah!

"Ta-dah!" said Baby Bear.
"There she is!"
And Goldilocks
was so startled,
she tumbled out
of bed.

U is for up.

Goldilocks jumped up.

V
is
for
very.

Goldilocks was
very,
very,
very,
very
frightened.

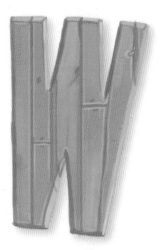

is window.

Goldilocks jumped
out the window.

X marks the exact spot where she landed.

Y is for yellow.

Yellow curls bobbed up and down
as Goldilocks bounced back up.
"YIKES!" yelled Goldilocks.

Z is for zipped.

Goldilocks zipped back home as fast as her legs could carry her.

And  is for zany . . .

because it was that kind of day!